Thomas Satchell, Leonard Mascall

A Booke of Fishing with Hooke and Line

Thomas Satchell, Leonard Mascall

A Booke of Fishing with Hooke and Line

ISBN/EAN: 9783337313319

Printed in Europe, USA, Canada, Australia, Japan

Cover: Foto ©Andreas Hilbeck / pixelio.de

More available books at **www.hansebooks.com**

A BOOKE OF FISHING

With Hooke and Line

MADE BY L.[EONARD] M.[ASCALL]

REPRINTED FROM THE EDITION

OF 1590

WITH PREFACE AND GLOSSARY

BY

THOMAS SATCHELL

Printed for

W. SATCHELL AND CO.

19, TAVISTOCK STREET

And sold by

SIMPKIN, MARSHALL, AND CO.

STATIONERS' HALL COURT

LONDON

1884

LONDON :

R. CLAY, SONS, AND TAYLOR,

BREAD STREET HILL.

PREFACE.

THE little black-letter volume here reprinted is very rare. Most of the copies which remain are now preserved in great libraries, and I am not aware that any example has been offered for sale for many years past.

The full title is as follows: "A Booke of fishing with Hooke & Line, and of all other instruments thereunto belonging. Another of sundrie Engines and Trapps to take Polecats, Buzards, Rattes, Mice and all other Kindes of Vermine and Beasts whatsoever, most profitable for all Warriners, and such as delight in this kinde of sport and pastime. Made by L. M. [Woodcut.] London Printed by John Wolfe, and are to be solde by Edwarde White dwelling at the little North doore of Paules at the sign of the Gunne. 1590." The first part ends with page 50. The second part has a fresh title-page, with a repetition of the woodcut. The pagination is continuous throughout. There are editions dated 1596, 1600, and 1606, but I have not had an opportunity of examining them. This "Booke of fishing with Hooke and Line" is a compilation made by a practical angler from the "Treatyse of fyshynge wyth an angle," from "L'agriculture et maison rustique" of Charles Estienne and other sources. The compiler, generally believed to be Leonard Mascall, has omitted the introductory portion of the "Treatyse," and some other paragraphs, but, with the exception of some corrections and additions, he has left the instructions as he found them.

The book is divided into 87 short chapters with headings similar to those used in the earlier form of the "Treatyse," and as these headings furnish a conspectus of the contents of the volume, and will facilitate a reference to it, they are here gathered together.

It will be noticed that the compiler, as previously stated, has omitted the
introductory passages in which angling is compared, to its advantage, with

hunting, hawking, and fowling, that he omits the directions for making rods and lines, and has rearranged the matter of the "Treatyse."

The chapters on the places and weather for angling, and on its "lets" or impediments; on the baits for particular fish; on artificial flies; on colouring lines; and on the selection of lines and plumbing them, are closely copied from the "Treatyse" of 1496, the variations in the language being only such as would be made by a transcriber who was himself practically acquainted with the Art. Occasionally, however, he allows himself greater licence, and adds to the instructions given in the "Treatyse." The chapter on the Carp has been rewritten, and its baits are specified, though the sentence, about being "loth to add more than I know and have proved," is preserved. The recent introduction of this fish is also here reasserted (and twice elsewhere in the book), but assumes this form: "The first bringer of them into England (as I have been credibly informed) was Master Mascoll of Plumsted in Sussex, who also brought first the planting of the Pippin in England." On the authority of this passage, Fuller assigns to Leonard Mascall the honour of first introducing the carp, and gives 1514 as the date of its introduction, but the assertion is refuted, as has been many times pointed out, by the fact that the "Treatyse," written certainly before 1496, and possibly before 1450, mentions this fish, and adds, "but there ben but fewe in England." Mascall may indeed have brought carp into the country, but he cannot be called the "first bringer of them."

How much of the rest of the book is the author's own and how much is drawn from other sources I have not been able precisely to ascertain, but Chapters (59) to (70) are, I find, taken from "L'agriculture et maison rustique de M. Charles Estienne, Docteur en Medecine" (liv. iv., chapters 13—18, 22—26), and the particular edition used appears to have been that: "A Paris, chez Jacques Du-Puys, 1570." This is inferred from the headings of the chapters

—not continued in later editions—which Mascall has preserved, and one of which has been curiously mistranslated. This is the chapter (66), p. 36, headed "To make it drie." The words in Estienne are "Pour les seiches "— to take "Crayfish."

Many of the miscellaneous paragraphs which complete the book are probably Mascall's own. They comprise the modes of capturing the otter and the water-rat, the heron, dabchick, and other birds preying on fish, breeding miller's thumbs and crayfish, bobbing for eels, making bird-lime, and, by way of conclusion, "a pretie way to take a pye."

But the most noticeable feature of the book is the writer's solicitude for "replenishing the waters," protecting the spawning fish, and putting down unfair weapons of destruction. To this subject he recurs again and again, and his heart is ever with his pen. In Chapter (77) "To breede millar's thumbes and loches," which is certainly his own, after telling us how fish "out of season are forbid to be taken and sold" in France, he adds emphatically: "I would to God it were so here with vs in England, and to haue more preseruers, and less spoylers of fish out of season and in season: then we should haue more plentie then we haue through this Realme. Also I would wish that all stoppe nets, and drags with casting nets, were banished in all common riuers throught this Realme for three moneths: as in March, Aprill, and May, wherein they take fish out of season as well as others, with great spoyles of spawne, both of great and small fish, for they vse such nets with small mesh, that kils all fish afore they come to any growth and good seruice for the common wealth" (p. 44). He adds that the "water Bayles" neglect their duties and allow the fishermen to do as they please, while the owners of the waters are equally indifferent, and extort such rents from the fishermen that the latter are compelled to take all the fish they can get. If "carefull men were put in office" he thinks we should have in the course of a few years "plentie of all riuer fish and also a great sparing of flesh."

In another place (p. 31), where he has added a page to a chapter taken from Estienne, he displays the spirit of a true sportsman, saying: "It is a good thing to haue plentie of fresh water fish, in riuers and pooles, and standing waters: and a great pleasure for man sometimes to take with his angle a dish of fish in those waters wherein fish is plentie and well preserued, not to vse any other engins, but with the hooke: and by such meanes as the lawes of this realme doth permit and allow, not to vse fire, handguns, crossebows, oyles, ointments, pouders, and pellets made to cast in the waters to stonny and poyson the fish, nor yet to vse all sorts of nets, and such as are deuourers of fish, as bow nets, casting nets, small trammels, shoue nets, and draught nets: which are destroyors of fish before they are growen to any bignesse." He proceeds to urge those taking the "government" of waters, "to replenish them with all such kinde of fish as may there be preserued and bred," and particularly recommends the "fenne pult," that is the Eel-pout or Burbot, found in the "fennes beside Peterborrow," as furnishing a "pleasant meate," and likely to do well in rivers and running waters. Yarrell, it may be observed, also thought that the Burbot has been undeservedly neglected as a food fish.

Leonard Mascall's book, it may be said in conclusion, is simply a collection of practical directions for the angler and fish preserver, such as a man of his time might prepare for his own use. The compiler indulges in no comments or reflections, save when his indignation as a propagator and protector of fish is roused by the doings of his neighbours. The passages from Estienne, some of which, such as the chapter on p. 35, "of the taking of fish," are singularly out of place, may have been added when the time came to him, as to other note-makers, of "making a book"; or they may have been added by another hand to eke out a volume, after Mascall's death.

I have again to thank the Rev. Professor Skeat for his kindness in looking over the Glossary, and supplying the valuable notes to which his name is attached.

DOWNSHIRE HILL, N.W.,
  March 19th, 1884.

A Booke of fishing

with Hooke and Line, and

of all other instruments there-

unto belonging.

* * * * *

London

Printed by John Wolfe, and are to be solde
by Edwarde White dwelling at the little North
doore of Paules at the signe of the Gunne.
1590.

First the knowledge of angling with the
Hooke and Lyne.

ERE will I declare briefly vnto you, how to angle with the hooke and lyne, in what times best, and in what places of the water to take fish. First in standing pooles, ye shall angle where the water is somthing déepe. There is no great choise of any place where it is any thing déepe, either in poole or other standing water: but in a riuer, ye shall angle best where it is déepe and cleare by the ground, being grauell or clay without any mudde or wéedes, and in whirling waters, or in a couert, as vnder a hollow banke or rootes of trées, or long wéedes floting aboue on the water, all these places are troublesome : also it is good angling in déepe stiffe streames, or in falles of waters or weares, and in fludde gates, and mill pooles, and it is good whereas the water resteth by the banke, or where the streame runneth nigh thereabout, being déepe and cleare by the ground, or any other place where ye may sée any fish houe aboue in the water, or hath any other féeding place to resort, or on that side the water where the winde hath no great power.

B

What times best to angle.

Here shall ye vnderstand what time of the day is best to angle, from the beginning of May vnto the moneth of September fish will byte.   The best angling to take fish, is earely in the morning from foure of the clock vntil it it be eight a clocke, other be méetly, but not so good as in the morning: also the cuenings be indifferent good to angle, if it be somewhat calme withall, or els not good, the winde blowing from the South or West.

Also if it be a cold whistling winde in a darke lowring day, for the darke lowring weather is much better to angle in : then in a cleare sunny day, and from the beginning of September vnto the end of Aprill, ye shall spare no time of the day to angle, and likewise many poole fish will byte best in the mid day about noone. If ye shall sée any time of the day, the Troute, or Grayling leape, ye may then angle to him a double worme, according to the same month, and if the water doth ebbe and flow, the fish in some place will byte best at the ebbe, and in some places at the floud, according to the places of rest, as behind pillers and arches of bridges, or such like suckering places in the most quiet water.

In what wether to angle in.

Here ye shall vnderstand in what wether ye shall best angle as aforesaide in the darke louring day, when the winde bloweth southly from the South or West : in the Summer season when the sunne is very hote, it is then naught to angle, but from September vnto Aprill, it is then good in a faire sunny day, the winde being then good : if it haue any part of the Orient or East, it is then naught to angle, for they will not byte, or when it is a great winde, snow, raine, or haile, or in a great tempest of thunder, or lightening, for it feareth them, or els in a swooly hote wether, all these times are not good to angle for to take fish.

Of twelue lets in taking fish.

Ye shall here vnderstand there be twelue manner of impediments or lets which causeth a man to take no fish, without other cunning that may happe by casualitie. The first is if your harnesse or lynes be not fitly made : the second is, if your baites be not good nor fine : the third is, when that ye angle not in the byting time : the fourth is, if that your fish be fearefull of the sight of man : the fift is, if the water be very thicke, white or redde by any floud late falen : the sixt is, if the fish for colde doe not stirre abroade : the seuenth is, if the wether then be too hote : the eight is, if it be in rainy wether : the nynth is, if then haile or snow do fall : the tenth is, if it be in any tempest : the eleuenth is, if then it be a great winde : the twelfth is, if the winde blow from the East, for that is worst, and commonly neither winter nor summer the fish will then byte : the West and South windes be good, but the South winde best of all.

To take the Salmon.

The Salmon is a gentle fish, but he is cumbrous to take : for commonly he is but in déepe places of great riuers, and commonly in the middest of the riuer : he is in season from March vnto Michaelmasse, and ye shall angle to him with a red worme, from the beginning to the ending, and with the bobbe worme that bréedeth in the dughill : also there is a soueraigne baite that bréedeth on the water docke : the Salmon byteth not at the ground but at the flote or aboue : ye may also take him with the dubbe worm at such time when he leapeth, but it hath seldom séene, and ye shall take him in like manner as ye doe take the Trout, or Grayling, or the Dace.

For the Troute.

The Troute is in season from March vnto Michaelmasse, he vseth commonly a cleane grauelly ground, and in a streame : ye may angle to him at all times with a ground lyne, lying or running, sauing in the leaping time, then with the dubbe flye, and earely in the morning with a running ground lyne, and further in the day with the flote lyne. Also yée may angle to him, in March with a Menowe hanged on your hooke by the nether parte without anye flote or plumbe, drawing it vppe and downe in the streame till ye féele him fast, but if ye angle to him with the flye, ye shall strike when he is a foote and more from your baite, for he commeth so fast ye may in the same time angle to him with a ground lyne, and bayted with a red worme, for that is a good sure baite, and is most vsed. Also in March, Aprill, May, September and October take the Menow on your hooke: in December, Januarie and Februarie drag with the bobworme at the ground: in June, July and August, fish with made flyes on your hooke: on the vpper part of the water, for that is a sure baite and is most vsed.

In Aprill take the red worme, and also of Juneba, otherwise called seuen eyes, or the great canker worme that brédeth in the bark of a great trée, and the red snaile. In May, take the stone flye or Caddis worme, and the bobbe worme vnder the Cowtorde: also ye may take the silke worme, and the baite that brédeth on a Fearne leafe.

In June take the red worme and nippe of his head, and put it on your hooke, and a codworme before. In July take the great red worme, and the codworme together. In August take the flesh flye, and the great red worme, and the fat of bacon, and binde it about your hooke. In September take the red worme, and the menow. In October, take the same, for they are speciall good for the Troute in all times of the yeare, from April vnto September, the Trout leapeth, then angle to him with a dubbed or armed hooke according to the saide monethes, for hée is strong in the water.

For the Grayling.

The Grayling, otherwise named Umbre, ye may angle for him as ye doe for the Troute, and these are commonly his baites: in March and in Aprill ye shall take the red worme: in May yée shall take the gréene worme, and asurall [a small] grayled worme, and the Docke canker, and the worme on the hawthorne : in June, the baite that bréedeth betwéene the barke and the tree of the Oke: in July, the baite that bréedeth on the Fearne leafe, and the great red worme, and nippe of his head, and put it on your hooke with the Codworme before: in August the red worme and the docke worme, and all the yeare after vse chiefly the red worme.

For the Barbyll.

The Barbell is a subtill and straunge fish to take, and very daintie to take his baite: these are commonly his baytes, in March and in Aprill ye shall angle to him with fresh chéese laide on a borde, and so cut [cut] it in small péeces square, the length of your hooke: then take a candle and burne it or smeare it on the end at the point of your hooke till it look yelow: then binde it on your hooke with Fletchers silke, and make it rough like a welbede worme, and this is verie good for all somer season: but in May and June ye shall take the Hawthorne worme, and the great redde worme before: in July the red worme for a chéefe baite, and the Hawthorne worme together, and also the worme that bréedeth in the water dog [? dock] leafe, and the yong Hornet worme together: in August and for all the yeare, take the tallow of a shéepe and soft chéese of each alike, and grinde or scrape them well and small together, till it waxe fine and tough, then put a little wheate flower, and make it into little pellets, and this is a good baite to angle at the bottom, and see that it doe sinke alone in the water, or els it is not good for this purpose.

The Carpe.

The Carpe also is a straunge and daintie fish to take, his baites are not well knowne, for he hath not long béene in this realme. The first bringer of them into England (as I have béene credibly enformed) was maister Mascoll of Plumsted in Sussex, who also brought first the planting of the Pippin in England: but now many places are replenished with Carpes, both in poundes and riuers, and because not knowing well his chéefe baites in each moneth, I will write the lesse of him, he is a straunge fish in the water, and very straunge to byte, but at certaine times to wit, at foure a clocke in the morning, and eight at night be his chiefe byting times, and he is so strong enarmed in the mouth, that no weake harnesse will hold him, and his byting is very tickle : but as touching his baytes, hauing small knowledge by experience, I am loth to write more then I know and haue prooued. But well I wote, the red worme and the Menow bée good baites for him in all times of the yeare, and in June with the cadys or water worme : in July, and in August with the Maggot or gentyll, and with the coale worme, also with paste made with hony and wheate flower, but in Automne, with the redde worme is best, and also the Grashopper with his legs cut off, which he wil take in the morning, or the whites of hard egges stéeped in tarte ale, or the white snaile.

The Cheuyn.

The Cheuyn is also a warie fish to take, and very fearefull : In March he will byte at the redde worme at the ground, for commonly he will byte at the ground, and somewhat déepe at all times of the yeare, in Aprill, the cadyce or ditch canker, and the canker that brédeth in the barke of a trée, and the worme that brédeth betwéene the barke and the Oke trée : also the red worme, and the young frogge his legges and féete cut off, also the stone Cadyce flye, and the bobbe worme vnder the cowturd, likewise the redde snaile : in May, the baite that brédeth on the Ozyar leafe, and the docke canker together put vpon your hooke, and the baite that brédeth on the ferne leafe, also the codde worme, and a baite that brédeth on the hawthorne, and the worme that brédeth on the oke leafe, and also the silke worme and the codde worme together : in June, take then the Crekets and the Dor flye, and also the red worme, the heade cut off, and a codde worme before, also the worme in the Oziar léefe, and young frogges, the féete cut off by the body or by the knée, also the baite on the hawthorne, and the codworme together, and the dunghill grubbe or worme and a great Grashopper : in July, the Grashopper, and the humble Bée in the medow the watcrest, also young wasps and white young Hornets, taken in their combes, and the greate branded flye that brédeth in pathes of medowes, and the flying Pysmyars, which be in the pismyar hilles : in August, take the

Colewort worme, and the Gentyll or Magot vntill Michaelmasse, and in September, take then the red worme, and these baites when ye may get them, which is, Cheries, young Myse not haired, and the sow worme that bréedeth in postes of the house.

The Breame

The Breame is a noble fish counted and a daintie, he is good to take, he is a strong fish in the water, ye shall angle to him from March vnto August with the redde worme, and then with the Butterflye, and the gréene flye, and also with the baite that bréedeth among gréene réede, and a worme that bréedeth in the barke of a dead trée, and to take young Bremets, take the Gentils or Maggots, and from August all the yeare after yée shall take the red worme, and if ye angle for him in the riuer, ye shall then take of browne bread, for that is good, yet some doe vse in Aprill and May, the worme that bréedeth on the Elme and willow, and chewed bread is very good, and all other baites vsed for the Cheuyn, but specially young waspes.

The Tench.

The Tench is a fish that féedeth at the bottom, and most part of the yeare among the mudde, and most he stirreth in the monethes of June and July, and in other times of the yeare but little : the Tench is an euill byter, and very subtill to take with the angle, his common baites are these, for all the yeare they take browne bread tosted and smeared with hony in likenesse of buttered toste, also they take the great red worme, and for a chiefe baite, take the blacke bloud in the hart of a shéepe, and mixe it with flower and hony, and temper them all together something softer then pappe or paste, and annoint therewith your red worme on your hooke : it is very good both for this kinde of fish, and for other also, and they will byte thereat much the better at all times.

To take Pearch.

The Perch is a daintie fish and passing wholesome for a man, he is also a free and greedy byter: these are his baites, in March they take the red worme, in Aprill, the bobbe worme vnder the cowdung, in May, the hawthorne worme and the codworme, in June the baite that bréedeth in an olde hollow oke, and the greater canker: in July the baite that bréedeth on the Ozier leafe, and the great bobbe-worme that bréedeth in the dunghill, and the flyeboate worme that bréedeth on the wéede raggewort, and the codworme: in August, then take the red worme and the Maggots or gentils, and the Menow tyed by the lippe, and for all the yeare after, ye shall take the red worme, for that is best.

The Roche.

The Roch is a wholesom fish and easie to take with the angle, for he is a ready byter: these are his baites: in March ye shall take the red worme, in Aprill, the bobbe worme vnder the cowdung, in May, the baite that bréedeth on the oke leafe and the flying Emmat, and the bobbe worme that bréedeth in the dunghill: in June the flying Ante, and the baite that bréedeth in the Ozier, and the cod-worme: in July, the worme in the flagge roote, and ye shall take of house flyes, and the baite that bréedeth on the oke, and the worme that bréedeth in the small nutte, and also the gentils, till Michaelmasse, and after Michaelmasse take the fatte of Bacon. Another speciall baite, take faire wheate and séeth it like furmantie: then take it out of the water and drie it, then frie it with hony, and good store of saffron, and then put it on your hooke, and the fish will byte thereat maruellous fast. But before ye angle, ye shall cast into the water a fewe crummes of bread, or take some crummes and fry them with some hony, and mixe it with saffron, and sée ye frie it not to much, for this is good and a chiefe baite.

The Dace.

The Dace is a gentle fish to take, and quicke at the bayte, hée biteth all the sommer nie the toppe of the water, and they angle to him without the flote in March, his bayte is the red worme, in Aprill, the bobbe worme vnder the cow-torde, in May, the docke cawker, and the bayte that is vnder the slowe thorne, and the worme on the oake leafe : in June, the codworme, and the bayte that bréedeth on the Ozyer, and the white worme in the dunghill : in July, then take house flyes, and the flyes that doe bréede in pysmyre hilles : also the codde worme and gentilles or magots, and those vse vntill Michaelmas, and if the water then be cleare, ye shall take fish when other take none : and from that time foorth, take baytes for him as ye do for the Roch, for commonly of their bayts and byting be all alike.

The Bleke.

The Bleke is a little fish in byting, and commonly hée bytes not nie the bottome, but aboue and in the middest of the water. His baytes from March to Michaelmas, are the same baytes which are written afore for the Roch. And also the Dace, sauing for all the sommer season, angle for him asmuch as you may with the house flie, and for the winter season, ye shall angle to him with Bakon flesh, and other baytes made méete for his purpose, as hereafter yée shall more vnderstande thereof.

The Ruffe.

The Ruffe is a holesome fish and good to byte, and ye shall angle to him with the same baytes, in all the moneths of the yeare, as I haue tolde you before of the Perch, for these two fishes are in eating and féeding all alike, sauing that the Ruffe is not so bigge as the Perch, for they are commonly alwayes lesse of growth, but the red worme is chiefe for them both.

The Flounder.

The Flounder is also a holesome fish for sicke folkes, and he will be in fresh waters and riuers, he is free in byting, but a subtill byter after his manner, in nibling long ere he take the bayte: and commonly when he sucketh his meate, he feedeth at the ground, and therefore ye must angle to him with a lying ground line: and they vse for him but one manner of bayte, which is the red worme, for that is the common and chiefest bayte for him, and all manner of fish.

The Googing.

The Googing is a good and a holesome fish, he is a readie byter, and byteth commonly at the ground, and his baytes through out the yeare are these: the red worme for the chiefest, also the codde worme and the gentell: and ye must angle to him with a flote or corke, and let alwayes your bayt be within two fingers or an inch of the bottome or lesse, or else for to dragge on the grounde, for so it is best and most soonest to take them. He vseth in deepe places with cleane sand or grauel ground at the bottome, as at wayers, bridges, and miltayles.

The Menow.

The Menow is a small fish and a bold byter, and byteth commonly at the bottome, as the Googine: it is a holesome fish to eate if he be gauld. For when he shineth in the water, he is then bitter, though his bodie be small: and he is a great rauening byter, and will have the bayte before other fish: ye shall angle to him with the same baytes as ye doe for the Gogin, sauing they must be small. And with a small hooke, or else ye shall often be deceiued by them: some angles to them with a line of two hookes or three, two together and on [an] other hooke aboue: they will be in all shalow places as in ditches, and such like.

The Yéele.

The Yéele is a gréedie fish, and hée byteth alwayes at the bottome, ye shall sée commonly holes in the bottom of the water, if ye put in your hooke there, yée shall soone haue him byte if he be there, and he will holde very harde a long time, ye must therefore holde your line stiffe, and hée will yéeld at length if ye plucke and striue with him hastely ye are like to loose him. And when he lyeth in a hole, it shall be best for to angle to him with your proch hooke, as is shewed after, but when you angle to the bottome for the Gogin, ye shall oft times take the Yéele when that he runneth abroad, as often they will specially in the euening. The great red worme is the chiefest bayte for him, or a Menow, or any péece of gutte, or such like.

The Pyke.

The Pyke is a common deuourer of most fish, where he cometh for to take him ye shall doe thus. Take a codling hooke, well armed with wyer, then take a small Roch or Gogin, or else a Frogge a line, or a fresh Hearing, and put through your armed wyer with your hooke on the end, and let your hooke rest in the mouth of your bayte, and out of the tayle thereof, and downe by the ridge or side of the fresh Hearing, and then put your line thereto, and drawe it vp and downe the water or poole, and if he sée it, hée will take it in haste, let him go with it a while, and then strike and holde, and so tyre him in the water. Some doe put the hooke in at the chéeke of the bayte, and foorth at the tayle : but when ye will lay your lyne, then must ye put a plummet of leade vpon your line, a yarde from your hooke, and a flote in the middest betwéene the leade and your bayte, that it sinke not to the bottome, for then the yéeles will eat your baite away. Ye may lay in your baites without flots, and often ye may spéede of pykes : and if you will sée a good sport in a pond where as there is store of Pykes, you shall put in a Goose, and put a frogge a liue on a hooke, and tye it with a strong pockthréed (to the Goose foote) a yeard long or more, and in short space ye shall sée good snatching and tugging betwéene the Pyke and the goose. An other maner of taking the Pyke there is : ye shall take a liue Frogge, and put him on your hooke at the necke betwéene the skinne and the bodie on the backe part, and put a flote as is aforesaide, then cast it in a riuer or pound, where ye thinke the Pyke haunteth, and ye shall soone take him : and the best laying or angling for him, is towardes night. Also another maner is to take him : take the same baite aforesaide, and put it into a safetida, and then cast it in the water with a long line and a hooke, and ye shall not fayle of him soone after.

An other baite for him : Take Boares grease a safetida, neppe, so boile alto gether, then take a Roch, or other small fish, and drie it in your bosome : and take and annoint him with the foresaide oyntment, and then put him on your hooke, and cast it into the water, and you shall spéede : also some doe vse to dragge for the Pyke with a bleke, Roch, or Gogin, in drawing it vp and downe the water, some-times aboue, and sometimes beneath, for so he will soonest come, if he sée it, and some anglers do put the hooke in at his gill, and out at his mouth, and so drawes the bayte, as though he did flie from the Pyke, which is taken for the better way to make him more eger to take it.

The Loch, and the Millers thumbe.

The Loch and the cull, or Miller's thumbe, they are good and wholesome fish, they féede at the bottome, and lye most part in wéedes, rootes, and holes in bankes, and to angle for them, ye must lay to the bottome, they do seldom byte at an hooke, but the red worme is their chiefest bayte that I do knowe for them, for their foode is commonly at the bottome, in sucking such as lies on the bottome of the water.

The manner of féeding and preserving your quicke baites.

Now I will tell you how you shall féepe [feede] and kéede [keepe] your quicke baites, which is, you shal féede and kéepe them al in general, but every maner by

him self, with such things as they bréede in, and vppon, and so long they be quicke
and newe, so long they are fine and good, but when they be once dead, they are
then nothing worth, out of these be excepted three broodes or kindes, that is to
wéete, of hornets, humble bées, and waspes, which ye shall take them after the
bread is drawen out of the ouen, and then dippe their heads in blood, and let them
so dry, and also for the magots when they be bred, and waxe great with their natural
féeding, yée shall continue and féede them, (furthermore) with shéepes tallowe, and
with a cake made of flower, and hony, which will cause them to be more greater,
and when ye haue cleansed them in a blanket bagge with sand, kéepe it hotte vnder
your gowne, or other warme thing two howers or three, then they wil be best to your
purpose, and ready for to angle with, and for the frog, when yée angle with him,
yée must cutte off his legges by the knées, and also the grasse-hopper, his legges and
winges by the body, all other made baites I will here let passe, but vse them as yée
thinke good.　　　　●

Baites to last all the yeare.

Here I will speake of certaine baites to last al the yéere. The first is made of
beane flowre, and leane fleshe of the hippes of a cony, or of a catte, with virgin waxe,
and shéepes tallow, so beate them in a morter, and then temper them at the fire,
with a litle clarified hony, and so make it vppe in small balles, and therewith yée may
baite your hooke according to the quantity, and this is a good baite for all manner
of fishe, that vseth the freshe waters.

Another.

Take the suet of a shéepe, and chéese, of each like quantity, and bray them
together long in a morter, then take flowre and temper it therewith, and then delay
it with hony, and so make balles thereof, and this is a special baite fo[r] the
barbell also.

Baites for fireat [*great*] *fishe.*

The baites for great fishe, yée shall kéepe in minde this rule, that is, whensouer yée doe take a great fishe, yée shall open the maw of him, and looke what yée finde therein, make that your baite for that time, for that is alwaies best and most surest. There is many other making of baites, but for lacke of knowledge therein, I wil here passe them ouer, and some not so néedefull as necessary as these aforesaide.

Of twelue kindes of made Flies to angle, for the trout, in Sommer with other fishe.

There hath béene vsed twelue maner of flyes, made and sette vnto the hookes to angle withall, on the top of the water, the which Flies are to angle for the grailing and darce, and chiefest for the troute, and also for the chub, like as now ye shall here me tell and declare, each by him selfe, the counterfeiting of them.

First for the dunne Fly.

1. The dun Fly (in March) the body is made of dunne woolle, and the winges of the partridge feathers.

2. Also there is another dunne Fly made, the body of blacke wooll, and the winges is made of the blacke drakes feathers, and of the feathers vnder the winges of his taile.

The stone Fly.

3. The stone Fly (in Aprill) the body is made of black wooll, made yellow vnder the winges, and vnder the tayl, and so made with the wings of the drake.

The ruddy Fly.

4. The ruddy Fly, in the beginning of May, is a good Fly to angle with aloft on the water, the body is made of redde wooll, lapt about with blacke silke, and the feathers of the winges of the drake, with the feathers of the red capons taile, or hakell.

The yellow Fly.

5. The yellow Fly (in May) is good, the body made of yellow wooll, and the winges made of the redde cockes hackell or taile, and of the drake littid, or coulered yellow.

The blacke Fly.

6. The blacke Fly or lowper (in May) the body is made of blacke wooll, and lapt about with the herle of the peacockes taile, the winges are made of the winges of a browne capon, with his blew feathers in the head.   .

The sad yellow Fly.

7. The sad yellow Fly (in June) the body is made of blacke wooll, with a yellow liste of either side, and the wings taken of the winges of the bozard, bound with blacke bracked hempe.

The More Fly.

8. The moorerish Fly is also good, made with the body of duskish wooll, and the winges made of the blaskishe male of the drake.

The tawny Fly.

9. The tawny Fly is good at Sainct Willams day, or vnto midde June, the body is made of tawny wooll, and the winges made contrary, one against the other, made of the whitishe maile of the wilde drake.

The waspe Fly.

10. The waspe Fly (in July) the body is made of black wooll, and lapped about with yellowe thréede, and the wings are made of the feathers of the bozard.

The shell Fly.

11. The shell Fly is good at Saint Thomas day, or midde July, the body is made of greene wooll, and lapped about with the herell of the peacocks taile, and the winges made of the winges of a bozard.

The darke or drake Fly.

12. The darke drake Fly (in August) is good, the body is made of blacke wooll, and lapped about with blacke silke, his winges are made of the maile of the black drake, with a blacke head. Thus are they made vpon the hooke, lapt about with some corke like each Fly afore mentioned.

Here followeth how to couller your lines, to
angle with.

Now to learne how to couler your lines of heare according to the couler of each water and season, in this wise, first yée shall take the haire of a white horse taile, the longest and strongest yée can get, the rounder haire the better it is. Then yée shall diuide it sixe partes, and yée shall couler each part by him selfe, as yellow, gréene, brown, tawny, russet, and the duske couler. And to make a good gréene, take a quart of small ale, and put it into a panne, and put thereto halfe a pound of alum, and so put therein your haire, and let it boile softly halfe a hower, then take forth the haire and let it drie, Then take a pottel of water and put it in a panne, and put therein too hand ful of Mary golds, or of wixen, and then presse it with a tile stone and so let it boile softly halfe a hower, and when the scum is yellow, then put in your haire, with halfe a pounde of coperes beaten into fine pouder, and so let it boile the space of halfe a mile way, then take it downe, and let it kéele the space of fiue or sixe howers, and so take forth your hair and drie it, which wilbe the finest gréene for the water, also the more of coperas yée doe put in it, the gréener it wilbe, or ye may put in stéed of it, verdigrece.

Another kinde to make another gréene, as thus, ye shal put your haire vnto a wood fatte, of plunket couler and it wilbe a light couler, and to make it plunket couler, then ye shall séeth it in goldes or wixen, like as I haue aforesaide, vnto this couler ye shall not put coperas, nor verdegrece, for it will doe better without.

To make yellow haire.

For to make yellow haire, ye shall séeth it with alum, as I haue afore shewed, and after that with goldes or wixen, without coperas or verdegrece. Also another yellow ye shall make thus. Take a pottell of small ale and stampe therein three handfull of gréene walnut leaues, so put them together, and lay your haire therein, so long till yée haue it so déepe couler as you desire.

To make a russet.

For to make your haire russet, yée shall take a pinte of strong ale, and halfe a pound of soote, with a little of the iuice of walnut leaues, and a quantitie of alum, then boile them well altogether in a panne, then take it off, and when it is colde, put therein your haire, and so let it lie till it be a darke couler, so as ye will haue it.

To make a browne couler.

For to make your browne couler, ye shall take a pound of soote and séeth it in a quart of ale, and with so many of walnut leaues, as ye shall thinke good, and when they shall waxe blacke, take it off the fire, and put therein your haire, and so let it lie still therein till it be as browne as yée will haue it. Also another browne couler, take of strong ale, and soote, and temper them altogether, and therein put your haire, and let it remaine so the space of two daies, and two nights, and it wilbe well.

To make a tawny haire.

For to make your haire a tawny couler, ye shall take a quantity of lime, with the like of water, and so put them together, and put your haire therein, and let it rest foure or fiue howers, then take it out, and put it in tannars ouse, for a day and it wilbe wel.

Also ye shall kéepe the first part of your haire white stil, for your lines to be reserued for the dubbid hooke, to fish for the troute, and grailing, and also to make small lines, to angle for the roche, and the darce, and such.

Lines fit for each water.

Here ye shall know in what water to angle, and for which season of the yeare your coulered lines will best serue.

The gréene colered line will serue in all cléere waters, from Aprill vnto September.

The yellow line is good to angle in euery water which is cleare, from September vnto November, for it wilbe like the wéedes, and other withered grasse which is in the water.

The russet line is best to angle withall in winter, and serueth best all the winter, vnto the end of Aprill, as well in riuers, as standing pooles.

The browne coulered line to angle withall, serueth for any water that is blacke, or of dedish couler, be it in riuers or standing waters.

Anglers and fishers.

The tawny coulered line to angle withal, serueth best for those waters that are heathy, or moorish couler. Thus much for your lines and cullers, practised according to the couler of waters, wishing that all anglers would not angle in vnseasonable times, as from midde March to mid May, for then is the chiefest spawning time, and increase of fishe. A great number there is in this realme which gouerns waters that spares no time to kill, nor cares for no time to saue, but takes at all times, which maketh fresh fishe so deare, and so scant in riuers and running waters. There is so many tillars, but few that seekes to saue and preserue them, they will not suffer the fishe so long as the time to spawne, but troubles the waters with nets and weles both night and day, and many Gentlemen lets their waters (as it should appeare) without any exception of times in the spring, for they make all times alike, not so much as sparing the spawning time, as March, Aprill, and May.

Thus much touching anglers, and all other fishermen, for these three moneths aforesaid, which I will speak more hereof in their places.

To order the red wormc.

When ye gather them, put them into a boxe or bag, with wet mosse vnder and aboue, and they wil store therein, then take and put them in parcely, fenell, margeram, if ye change them ech night and put them in new dung or earth, yée may so kéepe them good to angle sixe wéckes.

Here followetfi[eth] how to make your hookes.

If yée make your hookes of wier, it is the easier to cut the bord, with a hard
stéele knife and bend it (when ye have made the barbe and the point) with a paire
of plyars, or with an instrument, with a bowed wier in the end, and when ye haue
bowed him cut the shanke of what length ye thinke good, then batter him at the
end, and smooth it with your file, and it done, then heate him red in the fire, and
quenche him in colde water, and it wilbe hard againe, if it be a stéele nécdle ye
must holde it in the fire, till it be red hot, or ouer a candel, and then let it coole of
himselfe, and so it wilbe soft as wier, and to haue the knowlcdge of this instruments, and also how much your hookes and lines shalbe for euerie fish, here may
ye sée the figures of your instruments and hookes.

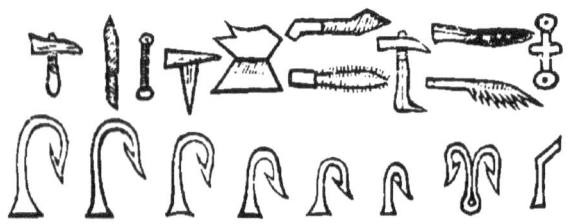

PIKE HOOKE, THE PROCH.

Now when ye haue made thus your hookes of al sorts, then must yée set them
to your lines, according in greatnes and strength, for euery fishe in this wise.   Ye
shall take small red silke, for a great hooke double, but twiste it not, and for small
hookes, let it be single, and therewith fret your hookes in doubling your lines end,
and your silke or haire on the inside of your double line, then fret or whippe it so
faire as yée shall sée good, then next your hooke at the bought put throw your silke
or haire in going round about the hooke thrée times, then plucke first your silke
or haire hard downe, and then your line, so cut it off harde by the end of your
hooke (in setting your line on the inside of your hooke,[)] and so it is done.

Now must yée know your hookes, how to angle for euerie kinde of fishe.

I will tell you with how many sufficient haires yée shall angle for euery kinde of fishe. For the Meno with a line of one haire, for the small or wexing roche, the bleke, the gagin, and the ruffe, with a line of two haires, for the darce and the great roche, with a line of three haire, for the perche, the flounder, and the small breme, with a line of foure haires, for the cheuin chubbe, the breme, the tenche, and the yéele, with a line of sixe haires, for the troute, the grailing, the barbyll, and the great cheuin, with a line of nine haires, for the great troute, with twelue haires, for the sawmon, with a line of fiftéene haires, and for the pike, a chalke line, and browne it with your browne couler aforesaid, and armed with a wier, as hereafter shalbe séene, when I speake of the pike.

To know how to plumbe your line.

Your lines must be plumbed with leade, finely and thin beate, and lapt close about your line next your hooke, and the next leade to your hooke must be from your hooke a foote long or else somewhat more : and euerie plummet ought to be of the quantitie according to his line in bignes. There be thrée maner of plummets and plumbings, which is for a groundline lying, and another for a groundline running : and the third line is the flote line set vpon the groundline lying, with ten plummets ioyning altogether, running vpon the ground with xx. or tenne tenne small plummets : and for the flote or corke line, leade or plumbe him so heauie, that the least plucke of any fish may plucke it downe, and make the leades or plummets sincke : for them, make them round and smooth, small and close to the line at both endes, that they fasten not on wéedes in the water, which will be a let to your angling, and for the more vnderstanding how they vse them, here shall be the figures.

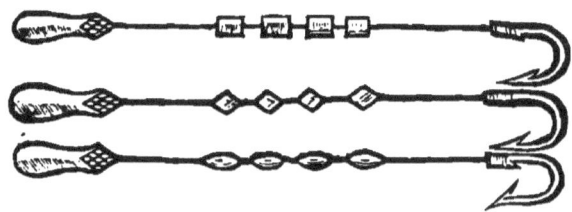

There is also a line without corke to fish with, which they vse in some places in sommer to angle for the Darce, the Bleke, and the Trowt, which they vse to cast his line into the water, and still to drawe the line, so that he may alwaies haue a sight thereof, and neuer let the hooke and bayte sinke to the bottome of the water out of sight: but alwaies casting and drawing or moouing the bayte, and kéeping it tight, that as soone as the fish doe bite, he giueth a tutch, and so kéepes his line tight and lets the fish tyre herselfe on the hooke, and then takes her vp gently, this is the chiefest way to have both line hooke and fish: for in snatching and striking hard when the fish bites, you put your line in daunger, or tearing the mouth of the fish and sometimes so loose him.

There is also an other kinde of angling for the Pyke, which is called dragging, your hooke béeing armed with wyer for shéering, when you would dragge for the Pyke, you shall take a small Roch, or a Gogin, and with a néedle of wood made thinne and flatte: put it in at the gille, betwixt the skinne and the bodie of the Roch, and so foorth at the taile, and drawe your armed wiar and hooke after, and place your hooke close vnder his gill, and so dragge for him as ye doe for the Darce. If it bée with a single hooke you shall put in your armed wiar at the mouth of the Roch or Gogin, and it will scrue well enough, as ye may here sée by figure, there is to drag with a line Frogge, and tie the double hooke vnder his necke and hippes.

Ye may if ye lust, place your double hooke at the mouth of your fish, as is declared of the single hooke : but then must you haue the bigger bayte, that the double hooke may lye or ioine close to the head of the baite, and then it will doe well.

THE SINGLE HOOKE.

THE DOUBLE HOOKE VNDER THE GILL.

THE ARMED HOOKE.

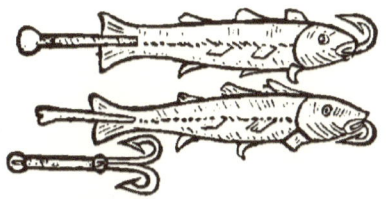

There is another kind of hooke, calde a proching hooke, which is made without a barke [barbe], this kinde or manner of hookes are to put in a hole in the banke, or betwixt two bordes at a bridge or water, or betwixt two stones where they lie open, for there commonly lieth the great Yeles, and there put in your proch hooke a little way, and if there bée any yéeles, they will take it anon : which proch, is wier whipt on a packethréedes ende, and couered with a great worme, and therewith prochin to the saide holes, asby example for the better vnderstanding, lo here you may sée the figures.

THE PROCH VNBAITED.

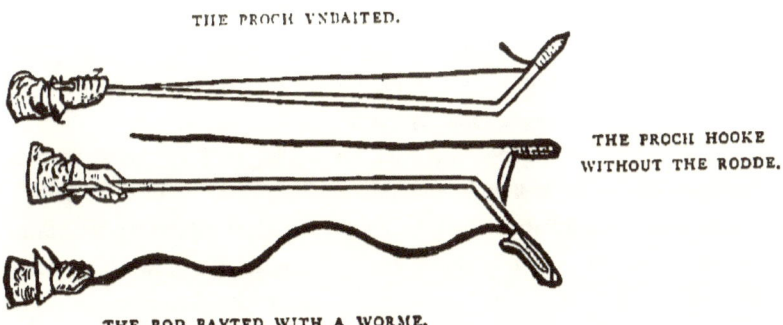

THE PROCH HOOKE
WITHOUT THE RODDE.

THE ROD BAYTED WITH A WORME.

As soone as ye féele she hath the baite, plucke away your rodde, for it doth nothing but guide your proch into ye holes, and then draw softly your packthréed line, and hold a while and he will yéelde, if you do plucke hastely, he will holde

so stiffe, ye shall breake your line, or teare his mouth : there holde hard still, and
at length he will yéelde, and come foorth.   And where ye shall sée any hole in the
bottome of a brooke or riuer, there is like to lie an yéele, put there in your proch,
and he will soone byte if he be there.   Thus much for the order of the proch hooke
to take the Yéele.

The manner of laying of hookes.

There is also a kind of laying of hookes armed for pikes, in pooles and riuers
ye shall bayte them as ye bayte the hooke in dragging for the Pyke : and here is to
be noted of two maner of layings of hookes, the one way is to the bottome of the
water without corke, and the other is with the flote or corke, to cast in your
bayted hooke without a corke, it will sinke to the bottome, and then the Yéele will
haue it as soone as the Pyke : and if he cannot swallow it, he will byte away the
baite by little and little : therefore to lay from the bottome is best for the Pyke, ye
shal cast your bayted hooke and line with a corke, of what depth ye lust, for so it
will not sinke to the bottome.

Also to lay for the yéeles, ye shall baite your hookes with menowes, gogins, or
loches, great wormes and such like.   And to sticke pooles in the bankes, with lines
at the endes so that your baites may lie on the bottome of the water, for there the
yéele will soonest take it, but lay not nigh roots of trées or such, for they will
wrappe them so, ye shall neuer come by them.

Also let your lines be of good great packthréeke[de], sticking the saide poles or
pinnes of wood in the bankes, and your lines to be of two or thrée fatham, some
more, some lesse : and for your proch hooke to baite him with the great worme, or
the menowe is best, or with a Loch, or small Gogin, so if a great yéele come, he
will swallowe it hole.   Thus much for laying of hookes for the Pyke and Yéele.

Also to take yéeles in winter, some haue vsed to lay in pondes or running
waters, faggots of hay, with a bough of Willow put in the middest, and bayted with
some garbage of foule or beastes, bound with two bondes, and to plucke it vp (after
it hath laine two or thrée daies) with hooke or corde, and you shall haue yéeles

therein : when it is a lande do but crush it with your foote and the yéeles will come out if there be any. If ye lay it in the middest of a riuer, you may plucke it into your boate. Thus you may take many yéeles in winter.

Here is how to saue and preserue fish.

For so much as I haue afore shewed certaine waies and practises how to take fish in riuers, pooles, and standing waters. I will here declare certaine waies how for to maintaine fish, and the chiefest waies to saue and preserue them in riuers, pooles, and standing waters, against such deuourers and rauerers [raueners] as hath and will destroy them, as Herne, the Dobchicke, the Coote, the Cormorant, the Sea-pie, the Kings fisher and such like : as also the Otter, which is a common destroier of pondes and standing waters, and a great deuourer of and spoyler of riuers, brookes, and running waters, which shall be declared in their places.

The Herne.

And first, to take the Hearne, which destroyes much young fish or other, if they come nigh the shallow places or bankes : the Hearne is fearefull and subtill for to take, therefore some do bayte a hooke, or proch hooke with a Menow or other small fish, or with the gobbet of some Yéele, then make your line gréene, or like the water where she hauntes in a shallow place or other where she resorts, there put in your pinne in the earth of the shallow water, and lay your baite so that she may wade halfe a féete déepe vnto it, for else the Kite or Crow will soone haue it, for she will soone swallow it and so be taken.

The Otter.

They take the Otter or water Wolfe, in a wele made and deuised for the nonce, as shall be shewed in his place, which wele is not made in all points like vnto other weles, where he will eate the fish and come foorth againe safe before he be drowned.

E

Therefore ther is inuented among the fisher men, a wele for to take him made with a double teme or tonnell, and against the vtmost teme within is set an yeirne like a gredyeirne with foure hooles staying and sliding vpon two round stickes, which must be set vpright in the wele before the teme, to holde vp the yeirne : which two stickes must be fast bound to the wele, both aboue and beneath, then must ye haue a good stiffe rod, the one ende shall be set ouer the wele to hold vp the gredyeirne or grate, and the other ende of the rodde, must reach ouer the inner teme, and a small oziar tied at the end of the rodde, which small Oziar must be made with a round knot, and so put downe vpon the ende of the nethermost Oziar in the midst of the inner teme, but a very litle way put on that when the Otter is within the first teme, he comes to the second where the fish is, and there he put off the Oziar, and the rodde flirtes vp, and the gredyerne falles and stoppes the vtmost teme where he came in, and as soone as he heares it fall, he will turn backe, without touching any fish, gnawing at the gredyerne where hée came in, and so is drowned.

And when ye haue a wele of fish robbed with the Otter, or your layer of weles with fish spoyled and robbed with the Otter, there lay your Otter Wele, well bayted with fish, and so ye shall soone take him. Which Otter Wele must be made of good round Ozyars of the Hasell rodde or gore rodde, for those are the best. These Otter Weles are made at Twyford, by sides Reading. There be two of the Gootheriches which liues much by making of such, and other weles. Also the Otter wele is made at Dorney, by Windsor, by one called Twiner. If your Otter wele be olde, and not strong, and if the Otter chaunce to breake it and scape, ye shall hardly take him of a long time after, for he is very subtill to be caught againe in such a wele. There be that hath prouided many wayes ere they could take him. Thus much héere for the setting of the Otter Wele, and here shall follow the saide Otter Wele, with his proportion how to be made and set, the more easier to make them where as they haue not béene scene before. To know if an Otter do haunt riuer or ponde, you must watch the waters in the night, then shall you heare him plunging and chasing the fish all night by efts and bankes sides, so watch or else your fish may be kilde and you know not how nor when.

Here followeth the Otter Wele.

The fashion of the Otter wele, with two handels aboue the better to lay him, he must be three quarters and more, betwixt teme, and teme in length.

This figure vnder shewes the setting of the gredyerne, before the teme of the

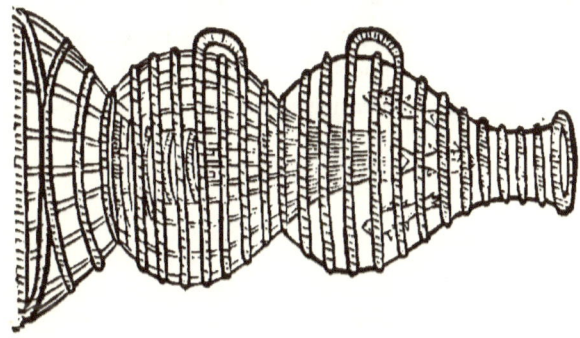

wele, and when he falles, to rest on two stiffe oziars on the lower part of the sayde teme, ye make sée aboue : but when ye shall set or tyle the saide gredyerne, it must be pluckt vppe aboue the mouth of the Teme, which temes mouth, all the oziars

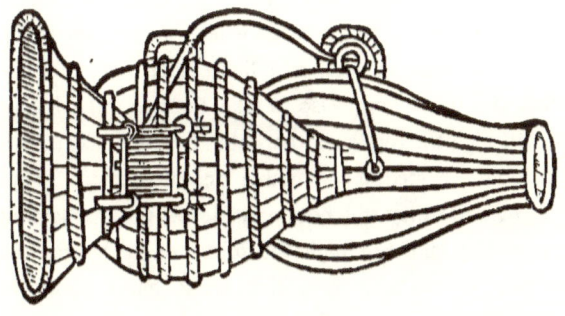

must be cut euen by the wreth, saue those two that must holde vp the gredyerne beneath as ye may sée. Which mouth of the teme, must be betwixt vi. and vij.

inches déepe, so that a good pretie dogge may créepe therein : for if it too little, the Otter will then gnaw the wele, also the gredyerne must fall easily on the two stickes that stay him, and the gredierne to be broder then the mouth of the teme, which gredierne must be put in the wele when the wele is a making, because it can not be put in whenit is made, except ye make it with playing ioyntes on the middle vane to folde, but on the one side of the gredierne, and so ye may set him in, and take him out when the wele is made, or when you will at any time. They do vse to make him without any ioyntes, but plaine and all flat barres, setting to foure round hoopes, of yeirne on the foure corners of the gredierne : which gredierne is made with fiue flat barres, and so vsed, waying about two pound weight, because it may fall the sooner.

For the Water-ratte.

The Water-rat is a hurtfull vermin to kill fish, especially Creuis, Loches, Culles, and Trowtes lying in holes of the banke. They will soone destroy much other fish and spaune in shallow riuers and brookes, to kill them it is hard to doe : but where as ye shall sée their path on bankes sides, there set a deadfall, for they do range abroad a nights like other Rats, and will be where as is corn milles, and fulling milles, to eate corne, and gnaw clothes, and liues much like to other Rattes, and will pill oziar barkes and such like. Also to take them in weles is hard, except the weles lie shallow, and nigh the toppe of the water by the banke : so a small Otter wele made for the nonce bayted, may possible deceiue them. They cannot tarrie long vnder water, wherefore they will not hunt déepe, nor robbe weles if they lie déepe, for they commonly take fish nigh the toppe of the water. But some men doe thinke a very good way to take them, that is : to pinne square bordes against the holes where they haunt, which bordes must haue a great hole in the middest, and set iust against her comming in or out, fast pinde to the bankes : then make a latch and set it on the out side of the borde, tyld as you tyle the Fore latch, as ye shall sée in his place : which hole in the borde on the nether part, ye shall set thrée or foure prickes of ozar to holde any thing that comes out or in. This practise may easely be made.

To lay poysoned baites, as péeces of chéese, flesh or such, and to straw the powder of Orsenike thereon, to be layde in efts, where other things come not. I knowe not what good it will doe, for whereas ye touch anything with your bare hande, they will not lightly come at it. Thus much for taking the water Rattes or Otter.

To preserue spawne in spawning time.

A chiefe way to saue spawne of fish, in March, Aprill, and May, is thus, ye shall make fagots of wheate, or ric strawe, all whole strawe not bruised, or of réede, binde these faggots together with thrée bondes, and all about thereon sticke of young branches of willowe. Then cast them in the water among wéedes, or by the bankes, and put in each faggot two good long stakes, driuen fast to the ground, and let your fagots lie couered in the water halfe a yeard or more. So the fish will come and shed their spawne thereon, and then it will quicken therein, so that no other fish can come to destroy or eate it, and as they waxe quicke they will come forth and saue themselues. Thus much for the preseruing of spawne in the spring and spawning time : this is a good practise to preserue the spawne of all scaled fish. These fagots ye may make and lay in all riuers, poundes, or standing waters. Your fagots had néede to be a yeard and a halfe long, and bound with thrée bandes not hard, two bandes a foote from the endes, and an other band in the middest, and lay them as I haue afore declared. Also some doe vse to hedge in corners in riuers and pondes with willow, and thereon fish doe cast their spawne and so bréedes.

The manner of way to take Sea-pies.

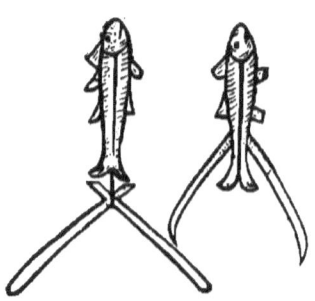

The Sea-pie is a foule that vseth the seas, and bréedes much in Ilands in the
sea, and liues most by fish and wormes, and where as they vse in fresh riuers, they
destroy much fish, young frie, and such as swimmes nigh the toppe of the water,
and will be in shallow places of the water: and there they haunt to take and féede
on them. Therefore the fisher men haue inuented a way howe to take them, which
is : ye shall lyme two small Oziars, and binde the ends that are next the bayte,
almost crosse wise. Then take an other short sticke, and binde the one end vnto
your ends of crosse twigges as ye may sée afore, and put that short sticke through
the fish or bayte. Then lay it on some water leafe, rushes, or such like in the
midst of the riuer, and as soone as they shall see it, they will take and flie away
with it in their bylles, and soone they shall be lymed therewith.

The other way of laying these limed twigges is, ye shall put a small short sticke
in the bayte, as yée may sée a fore. And at the hinder ende tye a thréed an intch
long, and to that thréed tie your lymed twigges, and when she takes and flies away
with it, she cannot flie farre but she will be lymed, for the twigs will turne and
touch her wings, and then she will fall. Thus ye may take many Sea-pies, both in
sommer and Winter, and the like way ye may take both Crowes and other Pyes,

to take the Kyte therewith, he will hardly be lymed, because he takes the bayte in his féete, and the other takes it in their billes. Thus much here for the taking of the Sea-pie.

Here shall follow the knowledge how to re-
plenish your fish pondes.

For to saue and maintaine in mayers, pooles, and standing waters, for such as haue not riuers, it shall be good to saue, kéepe, and maintaine all such fish as may be nourished and bred in fresh waters : as Pyke, Breame, Tench, Perch, Troute, Darce, Roch, and such like, and the Carpe for one of the best, which hath not béene here in Englande but of fewe yeares past. The Trout will not like but in running and swift waters, and hard grauell at the bottom. The slymie fish is the Tench, the Scacod, and the Yéele, and yet they are commended for a good féeding meat for man, but many will disdaine the fresh yéele, and estéeme it as a flaggie and slymie meate, saying : he will gender with the water snake, which thing possible may be, but the yéele of the fresh riuer is tryed a good and holsome meate, you shall haue also the Lampre, and the Lamporne, which are called venemous fish of the Sea, but when they haue scraped and clensed them in the fresh running waters. Notwithstanding, they are then good and holesome meat. The excrements of standing pooles are frogges, which in many places being well drest, they eate like fish, and is calde a kinde of fish, and doe taste aswell as a young poullet, for I tasted my part of many.

It is a good thing to haue plentie of fresh water fish, in riuers and pooles, and standing waters : and a great pleasure for man sometimes to take with his angle a dish of fish in those waters whereas fish is plentie and well preserued, not to vse any other engins, but with the hooke : and by such meanes as the lawes of this

realme doth permit and allow, not to vse fire, handguns, crossebowes, oyles, ointments, pouders, and pellets made to cast in the waters to stonny and poyson the
fish, nor yet to vse all sorts of nets, and such as are deuourers of fish, as bow nets,
casting nets, small trammels, shoue nets, and draught nets : which are destroyers of
fish before they are growen to any bignesse. These are not méete to be vsed but
of certaine Gentlemen in their seuerall waters, I would wish no running waters
should be let to any fisher man, without order what mesh, what nets, he or they shall
vse to fish with, and in what moneths of the yeare to refraine fishing, vpon paine to
forfaite his lease and all such engins.

Also it shall be good for all Gentlemen and others, hauing the gouernment of
any riuers, brookes, or standing pooles, to replenish them with all such kinde of
fish as may there be preserued or bred, aswell of straying as others. There is a
kinde of fish in Holand, in the fennes beside Peterborrow, which they call a poult,
they be like in making and greatnesse to the Whiting, but of the cullour of the
Loch : they come foorth of the fenne brookes, into the riuers nigh there about, as
in Wansworth riuer there are many of them. They stirre not all the sommer, but
in winter when it is most coldest weather. There they are taken at Milles in
Welles, and at wayers likewise. They are a pleasant meate, and some do thinke
they would be aswell in other riuers and running waters, as Huntington, Ware, and
such like, if those waters were replenished with them, as they may be with small
charge. They haue such plentie in the fenne brookes, they féede their hogges with
them. If other riuers were stored with them, it would be good for a common
wealth, as the Carpe which came of late yeares into England. Thus much for the
fenne pult.

Of clensing your pondes from wéedes.

If you will haue profite of your fish, in your pondes and pooles, ye must haue a care alwayes to clense them from thrée yeare to thrée yeare, in taking away all wéedes, rushes, and flagges, for they doe greatly stuffe and trouble the fish, and makes them to be more slymie, and of a worser taste. Likewise ye must sée alwayes for Otters and Water-rats, haunting your pondes and pooles: yée shall best know if there be any in the night season, for then they hunt abroad for fish : then séeke to take them by such means as afore mentioned, which else they will soone destroy all your fish. Also it is not good to suffer any to shute with guns nie your ponds and riuers, for it feares and astonish the fish greatly, and worst of all in spawning time, and many will die thereof : ye may watch the haunt of the Otter and Ratte, and strike them if yée can with the trowte speare, which is a very good thing to kill them, if it be well done, for so many haue béene kilde.

Here shall be shewed a care of lauing your pondes in sauing the water where it is scant for to saue your fish aliue.

In lauing your pondes and pooles, the greatest care is (if there be any scant of water) to kéepe and bestow it so, that the water which is cast foorth, may remaine nie the sides of your pondes and pooles, that ye may recouer it soone againe to saue the rest of your fish, while ye clense forth the wéedes and mudde, which will let the water to come quickly to the scoopes. Therefore it shall be best to clense the sides and bankes first of all : in hauing all such tooles readie, as shall be néedefull thereunto : as mattockes, spades, shoules, scauells, scoopes, and such like : to dispatch it as quickly as ye can. And when the water is lower than the Rat-hole in the bankes, ye may set such engins afore their holes to kill them at their comming out as afores-aide, for they will lye alwaies in the holes aboue the water, to smother

them in their holes ye shall hardly doe, if ye then let them scape, they will soone
conuay them selues away in the night or before night, and will runne very swift.
Thus much for lauing your pondes.

There is also a care alwayes to maintaine your pits and stuis with fish.

How your pits and stuis should be vsed to kéepe fish in, your stues and pits
ought to bée oft renued and helpt with great and small fish from time to time, and
refreshed often with small fish among : for if you doe alwaies take, and none put to,
your store shall soone decrease. It shall be good also to put carefully your fish
therein, both small and great, and sée that none be hurt if ye may, to put a Tench
with them it shall do well. And shall be very good husbandrie, to pricke and set
about the bandes [bankes], of willow, sallo, or alder, which will be good to defend
the heate in sommer, from your fish, and to auoide the colde in winter : but the
falling of leaues will increase mudde greatly, and also stinch your pondes.

How to nourish your fish in pooles, mayers, and standing waters.

It is most certaine, the fish which is in riuers, and running waters, are at more
libertie then those which are closed in pondes and pits : for those in running waters,
the water bringeth to them alwaies some what to féede on, and there also the small
fish doe nourish the great, but the fish inclosed can get no such thing. Therefore it
shalbe good to cast vnto them of small fish, and of guts and garbage of fish and of
beasts, and figges cut small, and nut curnels broosed, or broosed wheate, wormes,
graines of bruinges, white bread, all sortes of salt fishes cut and hackt in small péeces,
and such like. If your fish nourish and fat not with these, ye must féede them with
the frettes or gubbins of market fish of the fishmongers : if yet they be leane, it

shewes plaine they were taken from the seas, which fish are raueners, or they haue come from riuers nigh the seas, but the fish in pondes are restraint from these liberties. Therefore continually they must be fedde.

Of the taking of fish diuerse wayes.

There is diuerse maner of wayes in taking fish, in some places according to the Countrie, and the nature of great waters is one, and of riuers and pooles, is an other where they inhabite : so likewise is the diuersitie of the fish. Also in fishing, some manner of fishing is in the Seas, an other manner is in sweete waters, an other manner for great fish, an other manner for yeeles, other wayes for Roches and small fish, an other way for the Carpe, and such like. Now seeing there is so many diuersities in taking fish, it will be hard to expresse and long to write. Wherefore here I leaue that knowledge to those that vse to fish, and sell in markets. In speaking here in generall of the commodities for the father and his famelie, in taking of fish for the common wealth, whereof the principall maner is, with nets, weiles, lines and hookes. Thus I haue shewed of replenishing your pondes to haue plentie of fish, and clensing your pondes from weedes, and a care for your emptie pondes, and how to maintaine your pits and stues with fish. Also to nourish the fish in your standing waters, and declaring of diuers waies in taking of fish. Thus much taken of *Stephanus* in French.

Pour Amorcer, or gather Tortues.

Take Salarmoniacke eight drams, of Scalion Onions one dram, the fat of veale ten drams. So beate them together, and being made in pellets like beanes, cast them by their haunt to the Tortues, and they will come themselues to the smell thereof, and so ye may take them.

To make it drie.

Take the lées of strong wine mixt with oyle, and put it in a place where ye know it will drie, let it so remaine till it waxe blacke, and they will come to the place, where the ofle shall be put, and so ye may take them. Ye may take also Salarmoniack thirtéene drams, and the butter of goates milke eight drams, beate together, and make small soft pellets thereof, and therewith rubbe what graine, or small lynséede not broken, but dride : and they will féede there all about, and will not depart, and straite way ye may so take them.

To take Loches or small fish.

Take the branne of wheate meale, two pound, of lenten pease, halfe a pound, mixe them together, and beate them with a sufficient quantitie of brine, and put thereto halfe a pound of sessame. Then shall ye part it in péeces, and throw them here and there : for as soon as ye haue thrown it in the water, all the small fish will come vnto it, and remaine in one place, although they be 300. paces off. Also ye may take the bloud of an Oxe, Goate, Shéepe, or of a Hogge, with the dung that is in the small guts of them. Also of time, peniryall, léekes, saueric, margarum, garlick, with the lées of good wine, of each in like, with the grease or marow of the saide beastes, so much as ye séeme good : beate them a part, and then mixe them a like together, and so make small pellets thereof, and cast it where ye will haue the fish to come an houre before ye cast in your lines : or else take the bloud of a blacke Goate, the lées of good wine, of barley meale, all in like portion : beate them all together with the lites of a Goate, and then cut them in small péeces and make pellets therof, and so vse them as aboue sayde.

Another way.

Take halfe a pound of garlick, of burnt sessame as much, of pouliot, of organie, of time, great margerum, of sauerie, of wild stauisacre, of ech two and thirtie drams, of barley meale, one pound, of wheate as much, and of the barke of a Frankinsence trée thirtéen drams, worke all together with branne, and cast it to the fish, and they will assemble thereabout.

To take Perch.

The Perch is not so easily taken with hooke, nets, or bownet, but rather with proper baites made and vsed in a troubled water : therefore ye must make baites with the liuer of a Goate, and the snaile, or take the yellow butter flie which flyeth : of Goates whay, called *fromage de cheureau* of each foure drams, *opopauicis* two drams, hogges bloud foure drams, galbony foure drams, beate all well together, and sprincle it all ouer with pure wine, and make thereof small pellets, or as ye make perfumes, and drie them in the shade.

To take the Samon as well in the Riuer, as in the Sea.

Take eight drams of Cockes stones, and the curnels of pine apple trée burnt, sixtéene drams : beate all together a like, till it be in maner of a meale. Another. Take the séedes of wilde Rue, eight drams : the fat of a veale, eyght drams : of Sessame, thirtéene drams, beate all together, and make small loaues thereof, and vse them as the other before mentioned. Thus much more taken from *Stephanus* in French.

To take much fish by a light in the night.

Ye shall distill in a lembeck of glasse, a quantitie of glowormes that shineth at night, with a soft fire, and put the distilled water into a thin viall of glasse, and thereunto put foure ounces of quicksiluer, that must be purged or past thorough leather, or Kidde skinne. Then stoppe the glasse that no water enter, and tie it in the midst of your bow net for breaking, and so cast it in the water, and the fish will soone come vnto the light, and couet to enter into the net, and so ye shall take many. And some doth suppose if ye doe but take a certaine of those glowormes, and put them in a thinne viole or glasse, and then stoppe it close, and tie it in the net, then will shine as well and giue as much light. But then I doubt they will not long be aliue without meate, except ye put herbes vnto them in the day and let them féede, and vse them in the night as before. So yée may reserue them for your purpose (I thinke) a long time.

To take Yéeles in the winter in haye or straw bottles.

Ye shall make long fagots of hay, wrapt about willow boughes, which ye shall put in the midst of your bottle or faggot of hay, and then sinke it in the déepe by the banke, and so let it lie two or thrée dayes, and tie a wythe or rope thereunto that ye may soone plucke it vp on land or boate : and so ye shall take yéeles therein good store, in a colde weather very good. And if ye baite or lay in your faggotte guttes or garbedge of a beast, yée shall be the more certaine to haue them in a small time.

How to bréede and increase yéeles in riuers, pondes, and standing waters.

The common saying among fisher men is, if ye wil haue in your pits and pondes (being of a swéete water) great plentie of Yéeles in few yeares, ye shall digge two round or square turfes, whereon the dewe shewes most in the morning before the sunne doe rise. Then take them vp and clappe the gréene sides together one vpon another, and pin them fast together with prickes of wood. Then carrie and lay them softly in what pit or pond ye list, and ye shall sée experience. This is to be done in the moneth of May, by the dew then on the ground, and at no other time else of the yeare to be good.

The Gase for to catch Menowes.

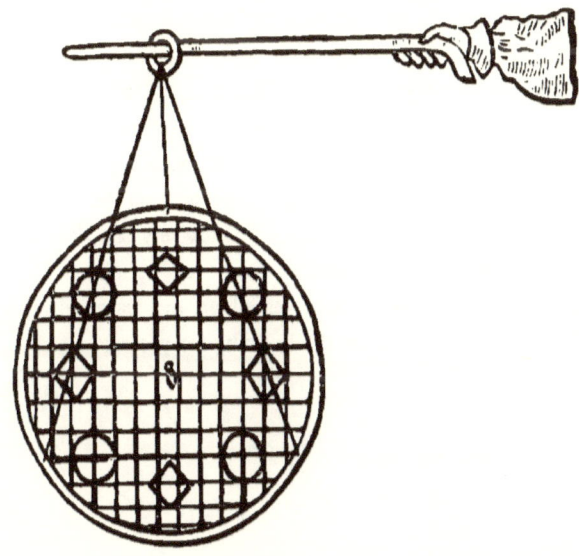

This Gase, is a round net of small mesh, with a hoope of yeirne, or great weir halfe an intch about, and to let sinke in a ditch, or brooke which is not déepe, and so holde it a while by thrée strings like a ballans, with a loope in the toppe, and therein to put through a staffe or poale, and yée shall haue within a while so many Menowes which will come and gase at it, as will couer it : ye must hang a small plommet in the middest, to make it sinke. And also the roundes must be flat oyster shelles tyde to, and the squares must be scarlet or red cloth sowed on : your hoope and net, may be thrée quarters and a halfe of a yeard broad from side to side. Thus much for the Gase.

How to bobbe for yéeles.

There is also a taking of yéeles with great wormes drawen through on a long thréede one by an other, and then feulded up thrée fingers déepe, and then tyde aboue all together, and a bigge string tide thereunto, and fastened vnto a short poale, which ye shall holde in your hand. This is vsed to bobbe at the comming of a floud water, and at the ebbing water of any water that ebbes and flowes. Also it is vsed after a great raine in brookes and running waters, ye must let your bobbe touch the bottome, and so vp with it softly againe, and so vse it still, and ye shall féele when any yéele doe bite : then pluck it vp not very fast, for then he will forsake the worme he hath hold of, and as soone as he féeles the ayre, he will léese his holde, therefore ye must haue a vessell on the water alwaies readie, that hée may fall therein. Thus much for the bobbing for yéeles.

The yeele speare to take yéeles.

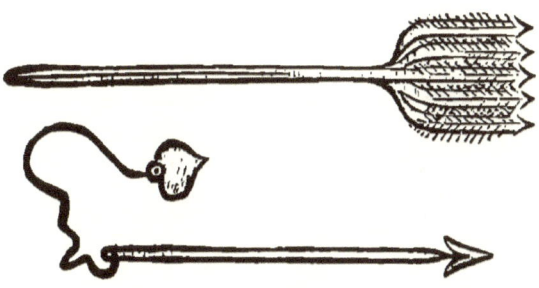

The Otter Speare.

The Yéele speare is made with fiue thinne barres, cut in the sides with téeth, to holde that yéele that is within them, and made with thicker and rounder plates aboue toward the socket, which socket must be made strong, and therein put your poale or staffe, which they vse in mudde, riuers, and brookes, to take a dish of yéeles at pleasure : but it is euill to vse the yéele speare whereas there is Teech [Tench], or Carpe, for they will commonly lie in the mudde when the water is beaten or troubled, and thereby they may soone be striken and die thereof.

The Otter speare is vsed when a man hunteth the Otter in riuers or brookes, when as a man shall chance to sée him vent aboue the water, then to throw the speare at him, which speare hath a line tide at the ende, and a small boxe fastened at the end of the line, that when yée haue stricken him, ye shall the sooner perceiue him where he diueth in the riuer.   Or if ye chaunce to finde him lying out of the water, there to strike him, and let him go into the water, and so kill him.

*To breede Millars-thumbes and Loches, in shallow
brookes or riuers.*

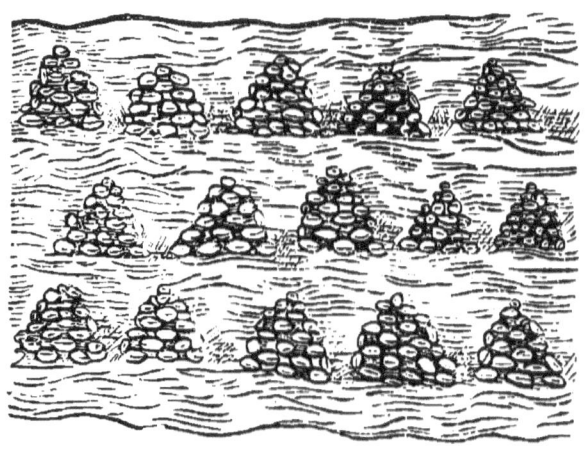

The fishes called Loches, and the other called Millars-thumbes or Culles, they
alwayes féede in the bottome of brookes, and riuers.   They are fish holesome to be
eaten of féeble persons hauing an ague, or other sicknesse.   These fish delight to be
in sandie grauell in riuers and brookes, and they are very easie to be taken with
small trauell, in remouing the stones where they lie vnder, for they cannot swim
fast away.   Therefore in certaine shallow riuers and brookes, they do vse to bréede,
and saue them ye may inlaying round heapes of pebble stones or flint, in shallow
places of the saide riuers and brookes, halfe a foote déepe of water or lesse.   Like
as there is a shallow riuer running from Barcamstede to Chestum, and so to Chauc :
also by Croydon and other places, wherein they might bréede of the saide fish
great store, if they were so giuen.   The like riuer runnes in Hampeshiere by sides
Altum, increasing by diuerse springes, and runnes shallow in many placed [places],

and by a certaine parish there called   the Parson thereof hath tolde me, he hath had so many of the saide Culles and Loches, to his tithe wéekely, that they haue founde him sufficient to eate Fridayes and Saterdayes, whereof he was called the Parson of Culles. This order of stones are laide hollow in shallow places lesse then halfe a foot déepe of water. Which fish among the saide heapes of stones doth there lie safe, and so bréedes: and there they are saued from the water Rats, and all other foules, which otherwise would still deuour them. These store of fish, men might haue in diuerse such like riuers in this Realm, if they would take the like paine, to lay such heapes of stones as is aboue set downe: which sheweth the maner of laying them round in the bottome, the circuit of two yeardes about, or as yée shall sée cause. Thus much I thought good to shew for the maintenance and bréeding of Culles and Loches. Also it is euident in other Countries, the great care they haue in preseruing their fish, especially in the spring: as in France, no fisher men or other, shall lay any engins in riuers or brookes in the night, as stewes, stalles, buckes, kéepes, weles, and such like, from mid March, to mid May: for then the fish doeth shed their spawne among wéedes and bushes, nor shall not beate the waters or brookes with any plonging poales, nor yet the fisher men to fish at no time, with any net vnder foure inches mash, because they shall not kill the small fish before they are well growen, vppon paine of forfaite and losse of all such engins. There is also prohibited, that no fish shall be taken and solde in markets, which are out of their season: as the Lampre and Lampornes, which are venemous in the Sea before they be scoured in fresh water, and not in season from mid March to mid September, for they will (being out of season) looke russet and speckled vpon their bellies. Also Oysters and Muskles, are not good from mid March, to mid September: and likewise Salmons and Trowtes, are in season from mid March to mid September, and after waxe out of season. Cockles and such are not kindly but in the monethes of March, Aprill and May: all the rest of the yeare not holesome to be eaten or solde. Moreouer Darce, Roch, Perch and such like, are not kindly to be kilde from mid March, to the end of May, for in these times they doe cast their spawne, and then they will be rough and broken, scaled and pilde for a while, after they haue so cast their spawne. And being then out of season, they are not so holesome nor yet good of liking. All these afore mentioned with all

other which are out of season, are forbid to be taken and solde in markets, or otherwise priuely eaten, vpon the like penaltie afore mentioned. I would to God it were
so here with vs in England, and to haue more preseruers, and lesse spoylers of fish
out of season and in season : then we should haue more plentie then we haue
through this Realme. Also I would wish that all stoppe nets, and drags with
casting nets, were banished in all common riuers throught this Realme for three
moneths : as in March, Aprill, and May, wherein they take fish out of season as
well as others, with great spoyles of spawne, both of great and small fish, for they
vse such nets with small mesh, that kils all fish afore they come to any growth and
good seruice for the common wealth. Who so euer doe preuent such, they shall
doe good to the common wealth. And water Bayles which are appointed to sée for
such nets in riuers, and running streames (which is thought) they neglect their duties,
for they let the fisher men vse what nets they list, as the voyce goes : and Gentlemen
which owes the waters lets them also alone, and the fisher men they say they pay
such rents, they must take what they can, so herein are none *yat* cares for the preseruing of the common wealth : whereby fish cannot increase, nor yet suffer to growe.
So I leaue, wishing that carefull men were put in office, and such as fauours the
common wealth, and all other put out that séekes for their owne profite onely.
Then should wée haue within fewe yeares, much plentie of all riuer fish, and also a
great sparing to flesh, if they would vse fish as they were woont on Frydayes,
Saterdayes, and fasting dayes commanded by our Prince, and so truely kept of all
people, from time to time.

The breeding of Creuis.

The fresh water Creuis, commonly liues and lyes in bankes and holes in riuers
and brookes, and they are a holesome fish for all sickne and weake persons. They
will cast their spawne in the spring about the moneth of May, and will shed it on
stones, and wéedes in the bottome, whereof most is eaten up with yéeles and water
rats, as some dò suppose. Therefore it were not vnméete to make fagots of hole
strawe to saue the spawne as aforesaide. Also they will soone be driuen with

flouds downe the streame, in few yeares they will greatly increase, if they be not taken with mens handes, and kild with Rats for they will lie in holes and vnder stones, and wéedes, and so are soone taken : for they cannot flie fast away. If they be taken in May, it will be a great spoyle of their increase, for commonly then they

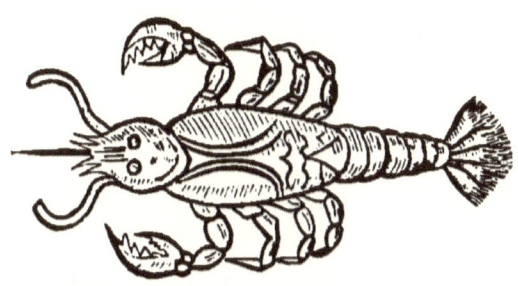

dœ shed their spawne. The Water-rat is also a great deuourer of them lying in holes : and whereas many rats are, they cannot lightly prosper or increase there. Thus much for the fresh water Creauis. Ye may store any brooke or riuer with the Creuis, but especially he loues the sandie and grauely running waters.

The Kinges fisher.

There is a bird which is a great destroyer of all young fry and small fish, and he is called the Kinges fisher : he is about the bignesse of a Larke, and doth commonly bréede in bankes, sides of riuers and brookes, in the spring of the yeare : his feathers are gréene and blewe, and he will alwayes haunt about the sides of riuers and brookes, whereas small fish is, and as soone as he hath caught a fish, he will straight way flie to the next bough, and there will sit on a twigge and eate the fish, and so fetch an other. Thus he liueth by the deuouring of all sortes of small frie, such as he may take and carrie away. For to take this birde, they vse to marke where his haunt is, and there they set downe a bush or branch, and they put a limed twigge vnder the saide bush or branch: for so soone as he hath taken a fish, he will flie to the next bush and light on that vnder twigge lymed, and so they take him. Also they say this bird, being dead, if he be hanged vp by the bill with a thréed in your house where no winde bloweth, his brest will alway hang against the winde, whereby ye may knowe perfectly in what quarter the winde is at all times, both night and day. Thus much of the bird called the Kings fisher.

The Cormorant.

The Cormorant is also a great destroyer of fish, hée vseth the fresh waters, and will diue vnder the water, and will take and eate fish of thrée and foure yeares growth. How to take or destroy them I know not well, otherwise then to destroy their nests in bréeding time, whereas they bréede in Ilands, and rockes by the sea: some may be destroyed in riuers and pooles, with crossebow, or hand gun, other wayes I haue not knowen or heard of, not with lime lines except it be in the night, and then they will pike them soone cleane againe.

The Dobchicke.

The Dobchicke is likewise a water fowle, and they will be alwayes commonly on riuers and pooles, and they are nigh as great as the Teales, and are of cullour blacke, and they will commonly diue vnder the water to take young fish, as I haue séene in riuers and brookes. Howe for to take them, the fisher men some doe vse to lay on the water long lines of small thréede knit full of little corkes, a handfull a sunder on the line, and cut foure square like bigge dice, and so limed and fold on aracle [a rackle], as I shall shewe hereafter: and where they sée them haunt, they will spread the saide line afore them on the water, and then with their boats, driue them to the sayd line, and so many are taken. Thus much for taking the Dobchickes.

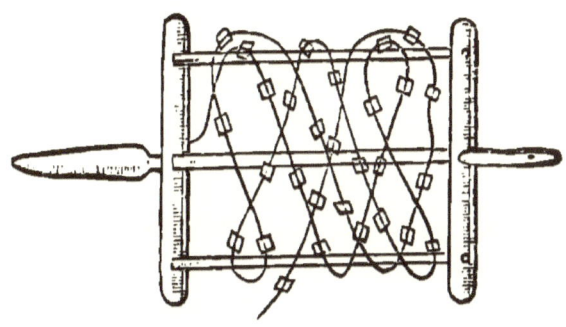

'This rackle, turnes rounde of the middle staffe, and as ye sée the thréed limed with small corkes, that is fold thereon, so long as ye shall haue it of length to lie on the water, and each corke to be but foure fingers a sunder, or lesse, shall suffice.

The More-coote or bauld Coote kils fish also.

The More henne or bauld coote, liues likewise on waters, and they also eat fish if they can take them. To kill or take these, I know no other way, but with lime, or with the gunne, or such like to kill them.

The making of a water lime, a verie good and a perfect way.

Ye shall first wash your birdlime in running water, that no knots be found therein, nor yet motes, but pike them out as cleane as ye can in the washing. Then take and boyle it in a pot or skillet, and in the boyling put in a little rosome, with some fresh grease, or goose grease, and so let it boyle softly a pretie space in storing it stil. Then take off the same lime, and put it to a weat testorne in water, if it come with the lime, it is good, if not, boyle it longer vntil ye sée that proofe. Also in stéede of rosom, ye may take white turpentine, for that is better. And this kinde of water lime, will holde both in water and frostie wether.

The Ospray.

The Ospray is a bird like a Hawke, nie as bigge as the Tarcell of a goshawke, he liueth by fish, and is a great destroyer of fish : for I haue séene him take fish in the middest of a great ponde, they say he hath one foote like a Ducke, and the other like a Hawke, and as he flies nie ouer the water, the fish will come vp vnto him. Howe to take him I know no other way but to watch where he prayes to eate his fish, for he will flie to some trée there aboutes, and there to kill him with the hand gunne, which I have séene in Hampshire. Thus much for the Ospray.

The tempering of bird-lime, and it will serue also well in water.

Take a pound of bird lime, cleanse and wash it in running water verie cleane that no knots be left therein. Then beate out the water and drie it againe. Then put thereto two spoonefuls of sharpe vinegar, and so much goose grease as will make it subtill to runne : and put therto halfe a spoonefull of lampe oyle, and a litle Venice Turpentine. Then boyle all these together in an earthen leaden panne, and sturre it alwayes, and let it but bubble and play softly. Then take it off the fire, and so reserue it and vse it at your pleasure, warme it when you will haue the vse thereof

Lime made of Misteltoo.

Dyoscorides sayth, they do gather the berries in Automne, in the full of the Moone, (for then they are of most force) and then they broose them, and so let them lie for a space and rotte, and then they wash them in running water, till they be cleane like other lime, and therewith they doe take birdes, as with other birde lime, made of Holly barkes.

A pretie way to take a Pye.

Ye shall lime a small thréede, a foote long or more, and then tie one end about a péece of flesh so bigge as shée may flie away withall: and at the other end of the thréed, tie a shoe buckle, and lay the flesh on a post, and let the thréede hang downe, and when she flies away with it, the thréede with the buckle will wrappe round her, and then she will fall, so ye may take them.

FINIS.

GLOSSARY.

BOUGHT, 20, *sb.*, the bend or loop of the line.

Bozard, 15, *sb.*, the buzzard.

Bracked, 15, *p.p.*, barked, stained with bark.

Branded, 6, *adj.*, brindled, streaked. Cf. brandling (Halliwell).

Creuis, creauis, 44, *sb.pl.*, crayfish.

Cull, 12, *sb.*, the miller's thumb, or bullhead (*Cottus gobio*).

Delay, 13, *v.*, to soften.

Dobchicke, 46, *sb.*, the dabchick.

Efts, 26, *sb.pl.*, probably the slack water under the tail-end of islands, &c. (Professor Skeat says, " I suspect *eft* to be the A.S. *æft*, aft.")

Fenne pult, 32, *sb.*, the burbot or eel-pout (*Lota vulgaris*).

Flaggie, 31, *adj.*, flabby, insipid.

Flirtes, 26, *v.*, springs up.

Frettes, 34, *sb.pl.*, trimmings of salt fish.

Furmantie, 8, *sb.*, frumenty or frumety, *i.e.* husked wheat boiled.

Gagin, 21, *sb.*, the gudgeon (*Gobio fluviatilis*).

Galbony, 37, *sb.*, galban or galbanum.

Gauld, 10, *p.p.*, galled, *i.e.*, with gall removed.

Gobbet, 25, *sb.*, a morsel.

Goldes, 17, *sb.pl.*, marigolds (*Calendula officinalis, L.*).

Googing, 10 ; gogin, 10 ; googine, 10, *sb.*, the gudgeon (*Gobio fluviatilis*).

Gore, 26, *sb.*, a spear, A.S., *gár*. (Professor Skeat suggests that the "gore rodde" or spear-shaft-rod, was probably of ash, seeing that the A.S. *æsc* means either ash or spear.)

Grayled, 4, probably an error for *brayled* (ringed), used in the 1496 edition of the "Treatyse." The first quarto has *braysed.*

Gredyeirne, 26, gredyerne, gredierne, *sb.*, gridiron.

Gubbins, 34, *sb.pl.*, trimmings of salt fish.

Halfe-a-mile-way, 17, = ten minutes.

Hove, 1, *v.*, to hover.

Iuneba, 4, *sb.*, the river lamprey (*Petromyzon fluviatilis*). This is probably the proper form of the word printed *Inneba* in the 1496 edition of the "Treatyse," but corrected to *Iuneba* in the subsequent quarto edition from the same press.

Lenten pease, 36, *lit.* spring peas.

Lets, 3, *sb.pl.*, impediments.

Littid, 15, *p.p.*, dyed. Icel. *lita*, to dye.

Lowper, 15, *sb.*, leaper.

Mayers, 31 and 34, probably a printer's error for *wayers*, weirs.

Moorish, 19, *adj.*, colour of peat.

Neppe, 12, *sb.*, cat-mint (*Nepeta cataria, L.*).

Ofle, 36, *sb.*, offal.

Opopauicis, 37, *sb.*, opopanax. (Mascall's printer has mistaken *n* for *u.*)

Organic, 37, *sb.*, marjoram (*Organum vulgare, L.*).

Plunket, 17, *sb.*, a kind of blue colour obtained from woad.

Pouliot, 37, *sb.*, penny-royal (*Mentha pulegium*). *Pouliot* is used by the French writer from whom

Mascall is translating, but was never an English name of the plant, though *Puliol royal* occurs in the old Herbals. Both names come from *pulegium*, and this from the fact (?) which Pliny mentions: "flos recentis inconsus palices necat odore" (Lib. xx., cap. xiv.).

Poult, 32, pult, 32, *sb.*, the burbot or eel-pout (*Lota vulgaris*).

Proch, 11, proching hooke, 23, *lit.* the hook pushed near. Fr. *proche.*

Racklè, 47, *sb.*, a small rack or frame with spindle for winding up a line.

Rosom, 49, *sb.*, resin.

Scauells, 33, *sb.pl.*, probably the same as the Suffolk word *scaffel* (Halliwell), a small spade used in draining, and having the edges slightly turned up.

Sheering, 22, *pr.p.*, shearing, cutting. ("For sheering," writes Professor Skeat, is "to prevent its being shorn or cut." In M.E., *for* has the very remarkable sense of "against" or "in order to prevent." "For percing of his herte" = to prevent his heart being pierced, is found in Chaucer's *Sir Thopas*.)

Shoules, 33, *sb.pl.*, shovels.

Sow-worme, 7, *sb.*, the wood-louse.

Stonny, 32, *v.* to stun.

Stuis, 34, *sb.pl.*, stews.

Suckering, 2, *pr.p.*, succouring, sheltering.

Swooly, 2, *adj.*, overpowering, sultry. *Sweal,* to burn.

Tarcell, 49, *sb.*, tercell, the male bird.

Teme, 26, *sb.*, an emptying-place, outlet. Cf. *teem* (Halliwell).

Testorne, 48, *sb.*, a testern, sixpence.

Tonnell, 26, *sb.*, a tunnel.

Tortues, 35, *French*, tortoises.

Tutch, 22, *sb.*, touch.

Tyle, 27, *v.*, to get ready, prepare. Cf. *teel*, to set a trap (Halliwell).

Weat, 48, *adj.*, wet.

Welbede, 5, *sb.*, whether a wood-louse, a centipede or millepede, I am uncertain. For the first, Mascall has *sow-worme*, but this word is his own, "rough like a welbede" coming from the first edition of the "Treatyse." "*Welbede* is evidently miswritten," notes Professor Skeat, "for *welbode*, and *bode* would be the old spelling of *bud*, which we have in *sharn-bud*." This word (?) under the form of *bug* has taken new root across the Atlantic, and appears to be applied to insects generally. Here, in one particular instance, both forms have survived: the *lady-bird*, i.e. *lady-bud*, is also called the *lady-bug*.

Wele, 27, *sb.*, a basket for catching fish.

Wixen, 17, *sb.*, greenweed (*Genista tinctoria*, L.).

Wood-fatte, 17, *sb.*, woad-vat.

Wreth, 27, *sb.*, a twisted band.

Yéele, 11, *sb.*, the eel.

Yeirne, 26, *sb.*, iron.